DAMIAN DROOTH SUPERSLEUTH

SPYCATCHER

by Barbara Mitchelhill

illustrated by Tony Ross

Librarian Reviewer
Joanne Bongaarts
Educational Consultant
MS in Library Media Education, Minnesota State University
Teacher and Media Specialist with Edina Public Schools, MN,
1993–2000

Reading Consultant
Elizabeth Stedem
Educator/Consultant, Colorado Springs, CO
MA in Elementary Education, University of Denver, CO

STONE ARCH BOOKS
Minneapolis   San Diego

First published in the United States in 2007
by Stone Arch Books,
151 Good Counsel Drive, P.O. Box 669,
Mankato, Minnesota 56002.
www.stonearchbooks.com

First published in 2006
by Andersen Press Ltd, London.

Library of Congress Cataloging-in-Publication Data
Mitchelhill, Barbara.
    Spycatcher / by Barbara Mitchelhill; illustrated by Tony Ross.
    p. cm. — (Pathway Books) (Damian Drooth Supersleuth)
    Summary: Young Damian Drooth goes after an industrial spy when a
local inventor reveals that his ideas are being stolen from the shed where he
works, perhaps by another inventor who has no ideas of his own.
    ISBN-13: 978-1-59889-121-8 (hardcover)
    ISBN-10: 1-59889-121-9 (hardcover)
    ISBN-13: 978-1-59889-266-6 (paperback)
    ISBN-10: 1-59889-266-5 (paperback)
    [1. Spies—Fiction. 2. Inventors—Fiction. 3. Mystery and detective
stories.] I. Ross, Tony, ill. II. Title. III. Series. IV. Series: Mitchelhill, Barbara.
Damian Drooth Supersleuth.
PZ7.M697Spy 2007
[Fic]—dc22   2006007181

Art Director: Heather Kindseth
Graphic Designer: Kay Fraser

1 2 3 4 5 6 11 10 09 08 07 06

Printed in the United States of America.

Table of Contents

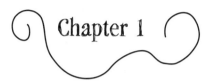

Chapter 1

You probably know my name. Damian Drooth, Supersleuth and Ace Detective. I've solved tons of crimes, but there was one big case that stands out. It involved big business, money, and lies and was really exciting.

As usual, Winston, Harry, Todd, and Lavender were gathered in my garden shed for detective school. Every week I gave them tips on how to solve crimes, for a fee of only one bag of chips.

That Saturday, Lavender was looking fed up, which wasn't like her.

Her mouth was all droopy and she wasn't listening as I taught them how to track criminals through a crowded store. All the other kids were really interested. Not Lavender.

"You look miserable, Lavender. What's up?" I asked.

For some reason, she burst into tears and all the boys turned to look at her.

"Don't worry, Damian," said Todd.

"My kid sister's always crying. I think girls do that. I don't know why."

We tried to keep going with the lesson, but Lavender was making so much noise that we could not even think. We had to stop.

"All right," said Todd, looking at his sister. "Tell us what's wrong or I'll take you back home."

She sniffled and said, "It's Mr. Swan. He's in terrible trouble."

"Mr. Swan?" I asked. "Who's he?"

"Mr. Swan is a very old man who lives by himself," Lavender said.

Todd explained that Lavender was talking about a man who lived on Water Street next to Todd and Lavender's grandma.

Lavender and Todd often visited the old man, who gave them treats and let them play in his yard. He didn't mind them playing in it because it was a little overgrown.

"So you get orange juice and cookies," I said. "What's the problem?"

"Now he gets very angry. He shouts at us. No orange juice. No cookies. He's really strange," said Lavender.

"Something must have happened. But I wonder what," I said.

"He won't tell us," said Lavender. "It's a mystery."

A mystery? Not for long, if I had anything to do with it.

Something spooky must have happened to Mr. Swan.

Like in that movie "Dr. Jekyll
and Mr. Hyde" where a man drinks
something that makes him change
into a monster. I just needed a little
time. I'd get to the bottom of it.

Chapter 2

I amazed the kids by working out a plan of action right away.

"You're so smart, Damian. You think of everything," said Lavender.

We disguised ourselves as gardeners (complete with gardening tools) and left the yard without Mom spotting us.

We headed for Water Street. When we got there, Lavender and Todd went to their grandma's house.

I knocked on Mr. Swan's front door with Winston and Harry standing behind me.

After a while, Mr. Swan unbolted the door and peeked out.

"Who are you?" he said in a crackly voice. "What do you want?"

Lavender was right. He was very old and very odd.

"We are a Help the Old Men Team," I said, "and we have come to weed your garden."

Mr. Swan laughed meanly. "Go away!" he said. He was about to slam the door but I jammed my shovel into the opening.

"We are here to help," I said, giving him one of my famous smiles. "The mayor sent us." This was a lie, but I was sure the mayor would approve.

"The mayor? Well," said Mr. Swan. He was thinking.

"We will do your weeding for free." I knew I was onto a good thing.

"Is that so?" he said. "I suppose it would be all right. You could trim some of the bushes, too."

He seemed to calm down then. He took us to the back yard and even brought out some orange juice and cookies. Things were going well.

The others started pulling out weeds while I interrogated Mr. Swan. ("Interrogated" is detective speak for getting people to answer questions.)

Mr. Swan told me that he was an inventor. Cool! I'd never met one before. But every time he had a new idea, it was stolen from his shed. Had he become so strange because he was worried about his work?

"I think another inventor in town is stealing my ideas," he told me. "They're jealous of my success. It's somebody who hasn't got any ideas of his own."

I had to agree that it made sense.

"I work in the shed so I've put locks on the door to keep him out," he said. "It's very important he doesn't get in before the Inventors' Competition. The plans have to be handed in on Monday. The prize is six thousand dollars."

Wow! That was a lot of money.
Then Mr. Swan suddenly had a violent
outburst. For no reason, he started
yelling at Harry and Winston.

"Stop! My roses!" he yelled. "My
bushes!" Mr. Swan started shaking his
stick, so we thought we'd better run for
it.

Chapter 3

Back at my shed, I told the gang what I had found out. "The fact is," I said, "Mr. Swan is upset because there's a spy in the neighborhood." They were shocked. A spy in our town!

"Spies go stealing other people's ideas," I explained. "They make lots of money selling the ideas to companies. It's called Industrial Espionage." I could tell they were impressed by my knowledge of the criminal world.

"You mean somebody's spying on Mr. Swan?" Lavender asked.

"Yes, Lavender," I said sadly.

We all thought that was unfair. No wonder Mr. Swan was upset. No wonder he was having temper tantrums and yelling at people.

But I had a great plan to track down whoever was doing the spying. And once I caught the spy, Mr. Swan would go back to being a friendly old man.

Early on in my detective career, I had noticed that there were certain kinds of people who are crooks for sure. These are the different types of criminals:

Criminal Type Number One: people whose eyes are close together.

Criminal Type Number Two: people with beards. These are usually men.

My plan was to walk up and down Water Street in disguise, looking for Criminal Types. This way I would prevent Mr. Swan's spy from breaking into his shed and taking his plans.

But Mom had other ideas. She was catering a big party that afternoon. She wanted me to go with her. Bad luck! I wanted to stay home.

"It's at the town hall and starts at four o'clock," she told me. "I need to be there at two to have enough time to put the food on the tables."

I tried to get out of it. "You go, Mom. I'll stay here."

She shook her head. "I don't think so, Damian. I am not leaving you home alone. I don't know what might happen. No. You'll have to come with me."

This was a problem. When spies are in the area, you have to act quickly. "But you say I always get into trouble when you're working," I said.

"You usually do, Damian. But you can stay in the kitchen. You can't get into much trouble there, can you?"

I tried everything but nothing worked. Mom insisted I take a shower and put clean clothes on. That's how serious she was.

This called for urgent action. The rest of the detective team had to be alerted. I needed to speak to Todd and give him the news. I turned the shower on so Mom would think I was in the bathroom. Then I went into her bedroom to use the phone.

"Todd," I said. "We've got an emergency. I can't work on the spy case this afternoon. I have to help Mom at the town hall. She can't manage without me."

Todd understood. He had a mom of his own and he knew all about helping out. Like when his bedroom needed straightening up and when the rabbit's cage needed cleaning out. He sometimes had to help her out then.

"What do you want me to do, Damian?" Todd asked.

I explained that I had divided the area around Water Street into three parts: one part for Harry, one for Winston and his dog Curly, and one for Todd and Lavender.

They were only beginner detectives so I couldn't expect them to patrol a big area.

"All you have to do is to walk around your own part of Water Street, keeping an eye open for anyone who looks like a spy," I said.

"Sounds simple," he said.

"Call the others, Todd, and tell them. Don't forget your notebook and wear a disguise."

"Okay," he said. "And I'll take Thumper with me."

That was good thinking, because his dog Thumper could smell a crook from a hundred feet away.

After I hung up the phone, I went back to the bathroom.

The shower was still running. But the drain hole was blocked and water was pouring out of the tub. I stayed calm and, to be helpful, I grabbed a couple of things to mop up the water.

How was I supposed to know that Mom wanted to wear that sweater to the party? It didn't look all that special to me. And it was perfect for mopping up water. She didn't have to shout at me. Sometimes I don't think anyone in our house notices when I help out.

Chapter 4

As I climbed into Mom's van, I felt depressed. The gang was going to do all the important work, while I was going to be stuck in a kitchen, probably washing the dishes.

This was bad news.

By the time we left, Mom had gotten over her bad mood about the sweater. She started telling me about the party. I wasn't interested.

Until she said, "The party's for all the inventors in the area."

Now I was interested. "Inventors?"

"Yes. Their club is called Inventors Anonymous," she said.

"What's anonymous mean?" I asked.

"It means your name is secret."

My spine began to tingle. Why would anyone want to keep their name secret? They must be up to no good.

"They meet once a month and they bring their latest inventions," said Mom, not knowing she was giving me vital information. "If you're good , I mean, really good, Damian, I'll ask if you can look at the inventions."

Would I be good? I'd be an angel if it meant I could meet the inventors.

For the rest of the ride I felt really excited. I even began to feel sorry for the other kids. They would be trudging through the streets looking for spies when all the time the spy would probably be at the party.

The Town Hall was a massive old building. We parked around the back and started to unload the van. "Don't touch a thing," said Mom. "I'll carry the food. Just follow me."

Mom worries about her cakes and stuff. She says I can't be trusted. She says I don't concentrate. She's wrong. I've only tripped a couple of times. Uneven sidewalks are not my fault.

We went down twisty hallways with stone floors until we reached the kitchen, which was big and old and smelled like cooked cabbage.

"You wait here, Damian, while I go back to get the rest of the things. And don't move!" said Mom.

It was a long way back to the van. Mom would be ten minutes at least. And the smell was making me feel dizzy. I needed to get a breath of fresh air, so I sneaked down the hall toward the front of the town hall, where I noticed that the floor was covered in red carpet. (A detective has to see everything.)

Unfortunately, just as I entered this interesting area, a huge man in a black suit blocked my way.

"Now, young man, where are you going?" he asked.

Quick as a flash, I said, "I'm looking for Inventors Anonymous."

He bent over, peered down at me, and scratched his chin.

"Aren't you a little young to be an inventor?" he asked.

"As a matter of fact," I said, keeping my cool, "I'm the youngest inventor in the area."

He shook his head.

"I thought the youngest one was Peter Parker. He's a genius and he's only sixteen. Are you Peter Parker?"

I pulled myself up to my full height. "I won't reveal my name," I said. "Don't you know that this club is called Inventors Anonymous? We keep our names secret."

That made him quiet. "I'm sorry," he said, looking upset. "Let me show you to the party room."

He took me over to a large oak door and pushed it open. "Excuse me, gentlemen, and um, lady, I believe I have one of your members here," said the man.

Everyone in the room turned to look at me. There were five men and one woman. They all had beards (Criminal Type Number Two).

Well, the woman didn't have a beard, but I noticed that her eyes were pretty close together (Criminal Type Number One).

In my experience, this meant that any one of them could be Mr. Swan's spy. What was I going to do?

A tall man with a shaggy, black beard came over. "Well, young man, who might you be?" he asked. I noticed that he didn't tell me his name. Neither would I.

I stuffed my hands in my pockets and looked down at the floor. My lips were sealed. I was not going to give away my real identity.

But Black Beard didn't give up. He kept trying to make me talk. "Come on, son. What's your name?"

The heat was on. The other inventors gathered around, grinning at me in a spooky kind of way, trying to make me talk.

Luckily, the door opened just then and everybody turned around to look.

"Ah, Peter, it's you," Black Beard called out as a teenage boy walked in. At once I guessed that he must be the genius, Peter Parker. At least he didn't have a beard.

He looked quite normal except for his very large glasses.

I scribbled his name on a piece of paper. It might be useful later. Who knows, Peter might be an example of Criminal Type Number Three: people wearing large glasses. I would wait and see if he behaved suspiciously.

"We've got a new member here, Peter," Black Beard said.

He pointed to me. "But he won't tell us his name. Can you find out?"

When I heard these words, I backed up against a wall, afraid that he was going to make me talk. I've seen spies torture people in movies just so they'll spill the beans. I didn't want it to happen to me.

"Stay away," I yelled. "Or I'll call the police."

"We only asked your name."

"Why do you need to know my name?" I asked.

"We just . . . ," started Black Beard.

"I won't tell you. I'll call Inspector Crockitt if you touch me. Help! Help!" I knew if I yelled loud enough someone would come to my rescue.

In just a few seconds, the door burst open and Mom rushed into the room.

Chapter 5

It turned out that when Mom explained the word "anonymous" she had gotten it wrong, sort of. The inventors were not "anonymous" at all. When I told them, they all laughed.

"No, we don't keep our names secret. That's just the name of our club," explained Black Beard.

Mom was not pleased. I guess she was upset that she had made a mistake. She tried to blame me, as usual.

"You shouldn't be here at all, Damian," she said. Her face turned bright red. "You promised that you'd stay in the kitchen."

"Now, now," said Black Beard (who told me his name was Albert Swindles), "I think the boy was just looking for some adventure. Let him stay with us while you're taking care of the food. He can look at our inventions. He won't get in any trouble here."

Mom tried to protest. She liked to keep an eye on me.

But Albert Swindles talked her into letting me stay.

I wrote down his name on the paper, and then wrote:

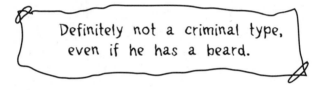

Definitely not a criminal type, even if he has a beard.

"Peter will look after him," he said. "He's a genius, you know. He's the top student in his class."

Mom is impressed by that kind of thing. Geniuses and good grades.

"Perhaps he can show Damian how important it is to work hard at school," she said. I just smiled and nodded. It's the only thing to do when grown-ups talk like that.

Once Mom left, I got down to serious detective work. After all, I was there to track down Mr. Swan's spy. Which of the inventors might have stolen his ideas?

I had another great plan. I would talk to each of them and try to trick them into revealing their criminal ways.

I got rid of Peter as fast as I could. He was only interested in setting up his Automatic Egg Boiling Machine, which is a crazy idea. Everybody knows how to boil an egg.

I walked around the room with my piece of paper, ready to take notes. I tried to talk to everybody, but I noticed that they all avoided answering my questions.

They said things like: "I'm busy," or "I've got a lot to do," or "Just leave me alone." Suspicious, I thought. The only one who would speak to me was the woman with eyes too close together.

She had finished setting up her Lemonade Maker, which looked very good. I was suddenly thirsty.

"Do you know Mr. Swan?" I asked.

She shook her head. "He used to come to our meetings, but he stopped coming a few months ago."

I scribbled down this interesting fact. I knew I was onto something. "Why did he stop coming?" I asked.

She blushed and looked kind of confused. "Well, he became a little strange. He thought people were stealing his ideas."

"And were they?" I asked.

She blushed even more. "Of course not," she said.

Was she telling the truth? That's what I wanted to know. Just as I was getting somewhere, Mom came in with a tray full of food that she set out on a huge table.

Everybody rushed to grab a plate, but I got to the front of the line.

I loaded my plate with sausage rolls and ham sandwiches and chips and my favorite, chocolate cake.

I went to sit over by the window. Peter Parker came to stand next to me. I even offered to finish his sandwiches. He handed me the plate and frowned as he stared at a paper he pulled from his pocket.

"Is that the plan for your next invention?" I asked.

"It's not finished yet," he said. "I only have one more day to get it right before the Inventors' Competition. The prize is six thousand dollars," he added.

I almost choked on my last egg salad sandwich. My detective's brain was racing.

I had forgotten about the competition. Now I knew for certain that I had found Mr. Swan's spy.

Chapter 6

When I got home that night, I called the kids in the detective school.

"I have serious news," I said. "Come to my shed tomorrow. 10 a.m. sharp. And by the way, don't forget to bring your detective notebooks."

The next morning, everybody wanted to tell me how their day of detecting had gone. It had been a rainy day.

"We got very wet, Damian," said Lavender, smiling at me.

"But we worked really hard," said Todd. "We saw a man with a beard on Mr. Swan's street."

"Criminal Type Number Two, Damian," said Lavender, bouncing up and down.

"We followed him up to Mr. Swan's door," said Winston. "We guessed he was going to break in so we tried to stop him. At least Thumper did."

"Good job!" I said.

"Not really. Our spy turned out to be the mailman," said Winston. I could see they had a lot to learn.

"He said he'd report us to the police," said Lavender.

"My mom'll go crazy if the police come after me," said Winston. "So we've decided we can't do any more detective work. It's too dangerous."

"Wait!" I said. "I've got something to tell you. I found the spy who stole Mr. Swan's plans."

I told them about Peter Parker, but it didn't make any difference. They didn't want to be involved with criminals. If I was going to catch Peter Parker, I was going to have to do it alone.

"There is one thing," I said.

"What?" Todd asked.

"I need to borrow a tent," I said.

"Why do you need a tent?"

"Today is the last day before the plans have to be handed in for the competition. Peter Parker will break into Mr. Swan's shed tonight, for sure. I have to be there, hiding. So I need a tent."

"You're so brave," said Lavender. "You can have my tent. It's really nice. It has fairies all over it."

I was horrified. Hiding out in a tent covered in fairies was not the right image for a detective. But nobody else had one, so what could I do?

My plan was this. Later that night, I would climb out of my bedroom window and slip over to Mr. Swan's house where I would wait. Then I would catch Peter Parker.

Chapter 7

I was pretending to watch TV with Mom, but I was really thinking about my plan to catch Mr. Swan's spy.
I had to go to bed as soon as possible because it was getting dark.

My detective's instinct told me that Peter Parker would strike soon, under cover of darkness. So I started to yawn.

"You look tired, Damian," said Mom.

"I think I'll go to bed early," I said. "I've got to be up early for school tomorrow."

"Have you done your homework?" she asked.

I sighed. Why is Mom so into homework? I use my brains in other ways.

"That Peter Parker is a smart boy," she said. "He must work very, very hard at school."

I couldn't tell her the truth, of course. I couldn't tell her he was a spy who stole other people's ideas.

I just said, "Some people are not what they seem to be, Mom."

She gave me one of her funny looks and turned the TV up. "Good night, Damian. Sleep well."

I raced upstairs and played around in the bathroom for a few minutes. I wanted her to think that everything was normal.

Then I went into my bedroom and changed into a pair of dark jeans, a black sweatshirt, and a baseball cap. It is important to be invisible when working at night, so I used a black marker to darken my face.

My eyeballs were showing up white. I fixed that by putting on a pair of dark sunglasses.

That was perfect, although I realized that it might be hard for me to see where I was going in the dark.

By eight o'clock, I knew I had to leave. Otherwise, I could be too late to catch the spy.

I pushed the window open, climbed out onto the roof of the kitchen, and jumped down.

Once I got to Mr. Swan's house, I quickly set up Lavender's tent in the front garden.

I put it next to the gate near a low stone wall. Nobody would notice it as they walked down the street, especially Peter Parker. I broke a few branches off some bushes and piled them on the tent. The disguise was great.

Lavender's tent was small. My feet stuck out at the end, but with the branches on top, I was cozy.

I closed my eyes. I decided to just listen for Mr. Swan's spy. I have excellent hearing.

Then the unexpected happened.

I was lying there near the gate when an elephant landed on top of me.

"Aaaahhhhgggg! Help!" I yelled. I couldn't get up.

I was squashed flat by the elephant's weight. I could hardly breathe.

The elephant screamed. "Oh no!"

Quick as a flash, I realized that elephants don't speak.

It must be Peter Parker!

I could feel him struggling, but he couldn't get up.

Some of the branches I had placed on the tent were very prickly and he was finding it hard to move. So was I! Using my fiercest voice, I shouted, "Don't think you can get away with this! You've been caught!"

"That's what you think!" he shouted back. Suddenly, I felt the weight of the master spy lift off of me. He was free and he was going to escape.

Chapter 8

Just at that moment, I heard two cars pull up. I could see that one had a flashing light on top. I struggled out of the tent and saw a shocking sight. Two policemen had arrived and were holding Albert Swindles!

It was obvious that they had made a stupid mistake. "You've got the wrong guy!" I yelled. "The real culprit has run off. This is Albert Swindles, the chairman of Inventors Anonymous."

"Damian! There you are!"

I looked over and saw Mom climbing out of her van with Lavender and Todd. "Oh, Damian," said Lavender as she ran to me and flung her arms around my waist. "We were very frightened when your mom called and said you weren't in your bed."

"She was really worried," said Todd.

"We had to tell her where you were. Sorry, Damian," Lavender said.

I understood. After all, they weren't trained in the art of keeping secrets.

Before Mom could yell at me,
Mr. Swan came out of the house in
his bathrobe. Todd's grandma came
from next door and most of the other
neighbors arrived at the same time.

They seemed really angry about
all the noise.

Mr. Swan was waving his stick at
the police officers.

"I called 911 ten minutes ago. Where have you been? I can't have crooks camping out in my garden. What are things coming to?"

I was standing in the middle of the noisy crowd, waiting to explain what I had been doing, when I noticed a clue.

Albert Swindles had something poking out of his pocket. It could only be Mr. Swan's plans.

Had my first guess about Albert Swindles been right after all? He did have a beard, a perfect match for Criminal Type Number Two. At the party on Saturday, he had been clever enough to cover up his unlawful activities by being friendly to me.

There were a lot of people and a lot of shouting and nobody seemed to want to hear my side of the story. Then another police car arrived. Out stepped Inspector Crockitt.

"What's this riot about?" he said to one of the officers. "What's going on?" Then he spotted me. "Damian!" he said.

I smiled and waved at him. Inspector Crockitt thinks I am a great help in the fight against crime.

I explained about Mr. Swan's spy. "He must have been around the back, breaking into the shed, while I was putting up my tent. He tripped over it on his way out." I pulled the paper from Albert Swindles's pocket and held it up for everyone to see before I continued. "And he got what he came for!"

Everyone gasped. Mr. Swan couldn't believe his eyes. He grabbed the paper and unfolded it. "These are the plans for my latest invention," he said. "Swindles has probably been stealing my ideas for months." Then he placed his hand on my shoulder. "This boy deserves a reward. He's better than all the police officers rolled up into one. He is a genius!"

Chapter 9

That is where my story ends. Except the part where Mr. Swan came in second in the Inventors' Competition and won $3,000. (Peter Parker won first prize, but we won't go into that.)

Mr. Swan spent some of the money on new roses and new bushes, and then he hired someone to help him with the weeding.

Everyone was expecting him to say, "Thank you very much for the prize," but he didn't. What he did say was a shock.

"The police in this town are
terrible," he said. "If you ask me, they
couldn't find their own heads."

"If you've got any problems," Mr. Swan continued, "you should ask Damian Drooth. He'll solve them for you. The boy is a genius!"

The audience cheered and wouldn't stop until I went up onto the stage. I didn't want to, but when you're famous you have to do these things.

"You are a hero, Damian," said Lavender, later. "Mr. Swan is his sweet old self again."

"Back to cookies and orange juice?"
I asked.

"Yes, Damian," she said. "Cookies
and orange juice, thanks to you!"

About the Author

Barbara Mitchelhill started writing when she was seven years old. She says, "When I was eight or nine, I used to pretend I was a detective, just like Damian. My friend, Liz, and I used to watch people walking down our street and we would write clues in our notebooks. I don't remember catching any criminals!" She has written many books for children. She lives in Shropshire, England, and gets some of her story ideas when she walks her dogs, Jeff and Ella.

About the Illustrator

Tony Ross was born in London in 1938. He has illustrated lots of books, including some by Paula Danziger, Michael Palin, and Roald Dahl. He also writes and illustrates his own books. He has worked as a cartoonist, graphic designer, and art director of an advertising agency. When he was a kid, he wanted to grow up to be a cowboy.

Glossary

anonymous (uh-NON-uh-muhss)—from or by a person whose identity is not known

blush (BLUHSH)—to become red in the face from embarrassment or shame

catering (KAY-tur-ing)—providing with food

concentrate (KON-suhn-trate)—to keep one's attention on something

culprit (KUHL-prit)—someone who is guilty of doing something wrong or illegal

depressed (di-PREST)—sad

detecting (di-TEK-ting)—doing detective work

genius (JEEN-yuhss)—someone who has great natural ability to think and create

inventor (in-VENT-er)—someone who creates or makes something new

spill the beans (SPILL thuh BEENZ)—to talk and give away a secret

suspicious (suh-SPISH-uhss)—acting in a way that makes others think something is wrong

Discussion Questions

1. Damian admits to telling lies. How do you feel about lying? Explain. What happens to Damian when he does tell lies?

2. Why is it important for an inventor to protect his work? Explain.

3. Damian tells his mother that "some people are not what they seem to be." What characters does this apply to in the book? Explain your thinking.

Writing Prompts

1. Damian likes to wear disguises. Describe the disguise you would have worn when dealing with Mr. Swan. Explain your thinking.

2. On page 43, Damian thinks for certain that he has discovered Mr. Swan's spy. Why does he think this? Who does he think it is? What clues is he using?

3. Write a detective story about a person breaking into a shed. Why are they breaking in? Is there something valuable inside? Explain how your detective would find clues and solve the mystery.

4. Write about an invention you would like to create. How would you make sure that no one steals your idea?

Internet Sites

Do you want to know more about subjects related to this book? Or are you interested in learning about other topics? Then check out FactHound, a fun, easy way to find Internet sites.

Our investigative staff has already sniffed out great sites for you!

Here's how to use FactHound:

1. Visit *www.facthound.com*

2. Select your grade level.

3. To learn more about subjects related to this book, type in the book's ISBN number: **1598891219**.

4. Click the **Fetch It** button.

FactHound will fetch the best Internet sites for you!